Riley Madison

Discovers the Superpower of a List

Hey Abby,
I hope
you enjoy
the book!
~Riley
Ahers

Abby, you love
I hope all about
reading Madison's crazy
Riley you use
day & that she
the "super power"
discovers too!

June
Ahers

Riley Madison

Discovers the Superpower of a List

Written by
JUNE AKERS

Illustrated by
RILEY AKERS

Published by Author Academy Elite
PO Box 43, Powell, OH 43065
www.AuthorAcademyElite.com

Identifiers:

LCCN: 2020920256
ISBN: 978-1-64746-569-8 (paperback)
ISBN: 978-1-64746-570-4 (hardback)
ISBN: 978-1-64746-571-1 (ebook)

Available in paperback, hardback, e-book, and audiobook

Dedication

For my daughter, the one and only Riley Madison. You are the inspiration for this book. Being your mom is an adventure. I'm so proud of the wonderful young lady you are becoming.

For my best friend, Brandon Akers. The man who inspires me to be my best and never quit. Thanks for ALL your support in EVERYTHING.

I love doing life with you.

Contents

Chapter 1

I Don't Want to Wake Up!

Beep! **Beep! BEEP!**

NO! Make it stop! It can't be morning already. I had such a hard time falling asleep last night because I was so excited about school starting. I am still so tired. My alarm clock must be broken. There is no way it's already time for school.

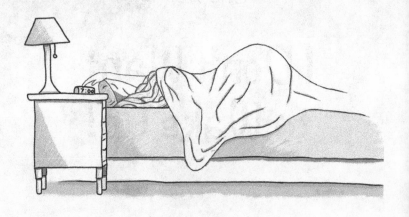

I quickly stick my arm out from under the covers and push the snooze button. I just need five more minutes, but what I really want is five more weeks of summer. Don't get me wrong, I like school. I love getting to see my friends. This year I actually got the teacher I wanted, Ms. Phipps. Everyone says she is so nice and super funny. I hope she will like me and not think that I talk too much like my other teachers did.

Actually, I am known for other things besides being a super talkative kid. People say I am nice, smart, clever, athletic, artistic, adventurous, and friendly. I really do love to talk though. It often gets me in trouble at school. Almost every report card says, "Riley Madison needs to focus on working quietly."

I just can't help it! I have so many thoughts, so many things to say. However, when it's recess or lunchtime and I actually *can* talk, I can't remember what I was going to say earlier. Of course, I can always think of many other things to talk about because my mind never stops.

Beep! **Beep! BEEP!**

I slowly slither my hand out from under the covers and turn off my annoying alarm. I really want to put my blankets back over my head, but I hear my mom on the stairs.

"Riley Madison, are you awake? Are you out of bed? If you are not out of that bed, you will be going to bed early tonight," she loudly says.

I know I should get up, but sometimes I don't always do what I know I am supposed to do.

Can you relate? Have you ever known you were supposed to do something, and you just didn't? I find myself in those situations a lot. Like one night, I was supposed to be getting ready for bed, but when I opened my toothbrush drawer, you are not going to believe what was in there. FACEPAINT! I excitedly pulled it out of the drawer. I love anything that has to do with paint. It is so fun!

Before I knew what had happened, I had painted a huge pink heart on my forehead, a colorful unicorn on the right side of my face, and a big yellow duck on the left side of my face. My nose felt left out, so I got some paint and colored it red like a clown. I thought my face looked amazing! Unfortunately, my mother did not. She was pretty upset that I had just gotten out of the shower, and rather than brushing my teeth to finish getting ready for bed, I had been doing art all over my face.

It's not that I am trying to disobey. I don't mean to not follow directions. I want to do what's right. I don't want people to think I am careless or forgetful, but sometimes my "racecar brain" takes over. When that happens, I lose my focus. I truly can't remember what I *am* supposed to be doing.

Creak! **Creak! CREAK!**

I hear my mom's footsteps in the hallway. "Riley Madison, if you aren't up, you aren't going to see what your first day of school surprise is," she says in a sing-song voice.

What? A surprise! I love surprises. I also love my sleep. Hmmm…do I want

to get the surprise? Do I want to get
more sleep? Well, I really want both,
but I have a choice to make.

What am I going to do?

Chapter 2

Getting Ready

I jump out of bed just before Mom opens the door. I am swaying a little bit because I got up way too fast. So, I put my hand on my bed to keep from falling and try to give mom the best fake awake smile ever.

Mom smiles at me sweetly and says, "Oh good, you are up! Way to make a great choice! Do you want to see your surprise?"

I eagerly nod my head up and down.

My mom brings her hands out from behind her back and says, "What do you think?"

I jump up and down and shout, "I love it!"

It is a lunchbox with cute little puppies all over it. It also has my name on it in big, blue letters. Maybe this is the year I won't lose my lunchbox.

"Now, get a move on. You don't want to be late on your first day of school. I am going to go and pack your favorite lunch while you get ready," Mom says.

I quickly turn around and start making up my bed. I know I said I wanted five more weeks of summer, but I am pretty excited about school starting. I just wish it started later in the day. I am not a fan of waking up early. I actually love school. I don't really have a favorite subject because I love learning about everything.

As I pick up the last pillow to finish making my bed, my mom yells, "Your breakfast is ready." What? She already has breakfast ready? I look down and realize that I am still in my pajamas.

I look in the mirror and realize my hair is sticking up everywhere. Yikes! I better hurry.

I open my closet door and stare at my clothes. Last night my mom said I should pick out my clothes and lay them out before I go to bed. That way I can get dressed faster, and I won't waste time in the morning deciding what to wear. I meant to do that, but I got distracted…again.

You see, I was about to go to bed last night when I remembered that I needed to pick out the outfit I wanted to wear on the first day of school. As

I looked in the closet, I spotted my cowgirl hat.

Immediately I grabbed the hat and plopped it on my head. My little brother, Lawson, walked by and said, "Hey! Let's play cowboys and cowgirls!" He ran off and put on his cowboy hat, along with his brown chaps and gun holsters. He came into my room with our stick horses, and as he handed one to me, he said, "Let's ride, Cowgirl!"

Lawson and I saddled up on our stick horses and galloped all around my room, through the playroom, into the kitchen, and then into Lawson's room. Just as we were about to gallop into our parents' room, my dad walked out and pretended to be the Tickle Monster. He said in his scary monster voice, "I'm going to get you!" Then, he started chasing us through the house!

When the Tickle Monster caught us, he tickled us until we couldn't breathe. When he finally stopped, he said, "Okay guys, it's time for bed."

I was so tired from galloping around the house and being tickled that I fell into my bed and went fast to sleep. I never thought about my first-day-of-school outfit again... until now.

Now my mom already has breakfast on the table, and I'm standing here staring in my closet looking for the perfect outfit. I have to hurry!

I quickly grab my favorite t-shirt. It is a superhero shirt that has a red cape you can attach to the back. I can't find the pants that match, so I decide to go with a pink skirt that looks like a tutu. I open my sock drawer, but I can't find a match. So, I grab one sock that has green hearts all over it and another one that has blue and yellow stripes.

I run to the bathroom and take another look at my hair. It is really messy this morning, so I quickly brush it. Unfortunately, my hair can't decide if it wants to be straight or curly. The top of my hair is very straight. However, underneath is curly and wavy. It's like this every morning. I really wish my hair would make a decision about whether it wants to be straight or curly!

What kind of hairstyle will go best with a superhero shirt, a tutu skirt, and nonmatching socks - a ponytail, braids, pigtails? What about a silly hairstyle, like what you do on crazy hair days at school? Maybe I could use my hair chalk and make blue and red streaks through my hair and then do two big funky pigtails.

What hairstyle should I choose?

Chapter 3

Morning Uh Oh's

"Riley! Where are you? Your breakfast is getting cold," my mom shouts up the stairs.

I really want to do the red and blue streaks and funky pigtails, but there isn't enough time. Maybe I can do that tomorrow. Today is definitely a ponytail day. I quickly brush my hair in a ponytail, wrap a red ribbon around it, and dash down the stairs.

My two little brothers are already sitting at the table finishing up their last few bites of breakfast. I sit down and start eating food as fast as I can.

Oh no...I just swallowed my food too fast, and it is stuck in my throat. I start coughing and gagging. My mom comes over to pat my back. I keep coughing and coughing. My baby brother, McGuire, starts laughing because he thinks I am trying to be funny. Then, uh oh...my food finally comes up and goes all over McGuire! He immediately stops laughing and looks up at Mom and me with his big blue eyes.

"WHHHHHHHHHAAAAAA!!!!!!!!! WHHHHHHHHAAAAAAAAA!" McGuire is crying loudly and looking at me like he might never forgive me. I cannot believe that I just threw up on the baby!

My dad comes to rescue McGuire, and Mom encourages me to drink some water and finish my breakfast. I scarf down the rest of my breakfast and run to put on my shoes.

Oh no! I was supposed to put my shoes by my backpack before I went upstairs to brush my teeth last night, but they aren't there. How did that happen? I remember going to the garage to get my shoes last night, but somehow, I forgot to actually get them.

Oh, now I remember. I opened the garage door to get my tennis shoes, but out of the corner of my eye I saw my sparkly hula-hoop. I grabbed it and started doing all my hula tricks. Of course, I can hula-hoop around my waist, and I can go forever. I can also hula-hoop around my neck, legs, and arms. I was having so much fun that I completely forgot about my shoes!

"Riley Madison, the bus is almost here. Let's go!" Mom says.

I dash out to the garage. Where are my tennis shoes? I can only find one of them. So, I decide to wear one tennis shoe on one foot and a cowgirl boot on the other.

I hear the bus coming down the road. I run to grab my backpack. I really hope my homework is in there. Wait! Did I even do my homework?

I run out the door. The bus is pulling up. "Stop! Don't leave without me!" I yell.

It's the first day of school. I can't miss the bus on the first day of school.

Is the bus driver going to wait for me?

Chapter 4

Emma
to the Rescue

The bus driver starts to pull away. I haven't even had time to put my backpack on my back. I am running with it in my hand, and my red cape is flying behind me like an actual superhero. Unfortunately, I'm not feeling very super heroic right now. I haven't had the best morning, and if the bus driver doesn't see me and stop the bus, my morning is going to get even worse.

Thankfully, I see the bus driver stop and turn the signal lights on. Whew! That was a close one.

The bus driver opens the door and kindly reminds me that I am supposed to be at the bus stop at least five minutes before the arrival time. I softly apologize and thank her for stopping. I hobble up the stairs and down the aisle of the bus to find my best friend, Emma.

Why am I hobbling rather than walking, you ask? Well, when you have a cowgirl boot on one foot and a tennis shoe on the other foot, it makes it hard to walk. You should try it. Then you will know exactly how I am walking, or rather hobbling, right now.

Emma looks up at me as I make my way to my seat. She starts to say hi, but her mouth just hangs wide-open. She is speechless. She looks at my hair that is now falling out of my ponytail since I had to make a run for the bus. Then she looks at my superhero shirt and cape. I realize she is probably thinking that a red superhero cape should not be worn with a pink tutu. Then she checks out my socks and asks me if I realize that they do not match. Last, she notices my shoes and says, "Oh my! Riley, what kind of fashion statement are you trying to make?"

I fill Emma in on how I got distracted and didn't have any of my clothes or even my shoes ready for the first day of school.

"Really? I have had my first day outfit picked out for two weeks," Emma responds.

I finally take a good look at Emma. She is wearing a rainbow dress, matching yellow socks, the same pair of light-up tennis shoes as me, but she has two of them that match. Her hair is perfectly straight, and she has a sparkly, colorful headband to match her dress.

Emma always looks so stylish. Her outfits are always matching, and kids always talk about how awesome her clothes are. Emma and I aren't very much alike. So, how did we end up as best friends?

Well, last year my dad got a new job, and our family had to move in the middle of the school year. I was really nervous about starting a new school and not knowing anyone.

The first morning I walked into my new school I got a little lost. Okay, I wasn't actually lost. I was curious. I knew where to go because my family and I visited earlier in the week. The guidance counselor showed us around the school, and my mom made sure I knew exactly where to find my class. So, I wasn't really lost.

You see, there was another door right beside my classroom door. I was curious as to what was behind the closed door. Rather than going into my classroom, I opened that door. It was dark. I couldn't see anything. I knew I should probably shut the door and go to my class, but I was so very curious.

I felt around on the wall and found the light switch. When the lights came on, I was in awe. I couldn't believe what I had just walked into. In the middle of the room was a round table and a chair. There was an art easel with paper on it ready to be painted. The walls were lined with all kinds of art supplies. There were markers, crayons, colored pencils, tons of PAINT, scissors, sharpened pencils, and so much more! I walked around the room and checked out all the art supplies. Then,

I went over to the easel. I just couldn't walk away from a blank piece of paper ready for a creation, could I? No, I could not.

I grabbed a pencil and started sketching. Before I knew it, I had drawn a picture of my bird, Spirit. Right when I finished the drawing, I heard the school bell ring. Ding, ding, ding. I hurriedly threw the pencil down and ran towards the door. I was late!

I tried to open the door, but it wouldn't open. I was locked inside! I started beating on the door and yelling, "Let me out! Let me out!"

The doorknob twisted and some-
one gently pushed open the door.

"You're not supposed to be in here,"
a voice whispered. "Are you okay?"

Emma was the one who opened the
door for me. She then quickly took
my hand and led me into the correct
classroom. When the teacher asked
where I had been, Emma sweetly said,
"She was lost, and I helped her find
the right classroom door."

I quickly looked at her and whispered, "Thank you. My name is Riley
Madison."

"I'm Emma," she whispered back.

Emma and I have been best friends ever since that day.

So now we are on our way to the first day of another school year. As the school bus starts slowing down to make a turn, Emma says, "Hey! Look! There is the school. I can't wait to see all our friends."

I look at Emma and then look down at my outfit. I am sort of wishing I could hide. I don't want to face all my friends yet. What will they be wearing? What will they say about my crazy clothes and mismatching shoes and socks?

Chapter 5

Classroom Distractions

"Wow! Riley, what an outfit." If I heard that one more time I was going to scream!

Emma and I speed walk to our new classroom. We are super excited to be in the same class again.

Ms. Phipps greets us at the door with a beautiful smile and welcomes us to her class. Then she hands us a piece of paper and sweetly says, "Here is your checklist for this morning, girls. Please read it carefully and check off every box."

I skip into my new class. I look around and see that Ms. Phipps has chosen an ocean theme for our classroom. There are fish and sea creatures on book boxes, whales and bubbles hanging from the ceiling, and dolphins on posters that teach us all about nouns and verbs. There are even fish on our desks that have our name and student

number. Sea creatures are everywhere!
It looks really cool.

As I am examining an octopus, I
notice my friend Cohen. I run over to
her to ask how her summer went and
what all she did. After I catch up with
Cohen, I see all the classroom books
that are available for us to read. I walk
over and start looking through them.
I love to read. Once I start reading, I
get lost in the book and don't hear or
notice anything else that is going on
around me.

After I browse through the books,
I see an art easel. Ms. Phipps doesn't
have anything on it, so I decide I will

surprise my teacher with a beautiful sketch. I sit down and begin sketching Ms. Phipps. I decide to do it in a cartoon character style. Just as I am putting the final touches on my creation, Ms. Phipps walks over.

"Wow! Riley, is that a picture of me?" she asks.

I proudly nod my head.

"Thank you for drawing a picture of me. You are quite an artist!" she says. "I was wondering if you have finished your morning checklist though?"

Whoops! Oh no! The checklist! When I walked into the classroom, I got so distracted that I completely forgot about it.

"I will get to that right now," I tell Ms. Phipps.

Where is the checklist? Wait? Where is my backpack and lunchbox? What did I do with everything?

I think back to retrace my steps. When I first came into the classroom, I walked around looking at all the fish. I do a quick scan of the classroom floor and see my backpack and lunchbox over in the book section of our room.

I must have sat it there when I was browsing through all the books.

I quickly walk over to grab my lunchbox and backpack hoping that the checklist is there too. When I pick up my stuff there is no checklist to be found. Where did it go? I look around all the books. I look around Cohen's desk. I go to the art easel, but no, the checklist isn't anywhere.

"Looking for this?" Emma asks.

"Yes, thanks," I whisper, and I quickly breathe a sigh of relief. "Did you already finish checking off the boxes on your checklist?"

"I sure did," Emma proudly says. "I am now on the checkbox that says to pick a book and enjoy reading on your own."

I was so jealous. I would love nothing more than to go pick a good book and just sit down and read, but I have a checklist to work on. Hopefully I can check things off quickly and have time to read before the morning school bell rings.

Ding, ding, ding! The bell is ringing already? I am still standing back in the book section, holding my backpack and lunchbox and a checklist that doesn't have **ONE** thing checked off. Yikes!

Ms. Phipps asks everyone to please find their seat and pay attention to the morning announcements.

I don't even know where my seat is. I spot Emma looking at me and pointing at the empty desk beside her.

I hurry to my desk. Unfortunately, I haven't hung up my backpack or lunchbox, so I try to sit in my desk with all my stuff. It is pretty uncomfortable. I look around and realize that everyone is sitting in their desk like normal people. No one else has things crowding their desk. I guess they all finished their checklists.

As I listen to the morning announcements, I try to figure out a way to sit more comfortably with all my stuff. I move my backpack to hang on the back of my chair. However, it is so heavy it makes my chair fall over. The loud thud makes everyone turn to look at me.

"Riley Madison, can you please make sure you are focusing on the morning announcements?" Ms. Phipps asks.

I put my backpack on top of my desk and sit in my chair, but now I can't see the announcements over my backpack.

So, I put my backpack in the chair, and I sit on the desk.

The kid behind me whispers, "Riley Madison, I can't see the announcements. You are too tall!"

I duck down, but that's not comfortable either. I remember one time I saw this kid laying on top of his desk doing what looked like a backstretch.

Hey! Maybe I'll try that. Then, the kid behind me can see, and I can stretch my back too.

I lay down on top of my desk with my legs hanging off one side and my head hanging off the other side with my arms dangling down to the ground.

Wow! This really does stretch your back.

I continue to watch the announcements in my stretchy back position. Once they are over, I try to get up. As I stand up, I start to feel dizzy, everything turns black, and I start falling to the floor.

What is happening to me?

Chapter 6

The Power
of a Checklist

I open my eyes and see Ms. Phipps standing above me along with all the other kids in my class. Everyone has concerned faces as they look down at me sprawled out on the floor.

What is that weird thing I am feeling under my booty? Oh no, it feels like…it isn't…it can't be…I am sitting on top of my lunchbox! Oh great! Now I will be eating a smashed sandwich and crumbled up chips for lunch. Thanks to my booty finding my lunchbox for its landing.

"Riley Madison, are you okay?" Ms. Phipps worriedly asks.

I wiggle my hands, my arms, my legs, my feet, and my head. I would wiggle my booty, but I don't want my lunch to be smashed any more than it already is.

I smile up at Ms. Phipps and all my classmates. I am embarrassed, but I let them know that I can move everything. Well, I don't know about my booty, but I am not taking a chance on that.

Emma offers me her hand and helps me up. As I stand up, Ms. Phipps notices my backpack, lunchbox, and **un**checked checklist.

She gives a small smile to everyone and says, "I know today is your first day of school. From now on, when the bell rings each morning, I want everyone to have their things unpacked and be ready to learn once the announcements are over. However, I am going to give you all a few more minutes today to make sure everyone has finished their checklist."

I give her the biggest smile ever! I really need a few more minutes to complete my checklist.

I walk over to my checklist and look at the first box. Checkbox one – "Unpack your school supplies and put them in the labeled boxes at the front of the classroom." I grab my school supplies and walk over to the boxes. I place the crayons in the big crayon box, scissors in the labeled scissor box, markers, Kleenex, glue... It's quite a lot of stuff, but I finally get everything put away correctly.

I go back to my checklist and look at Checkbox two. "Put your backpack and lunchbox in your cubby." I walk over and find my cubby that's decorated with a big goldfish that has my name and student number. I neatly hang up my backpack and lunchbox.

I am feeling quite good checking off this checklist. Let's see, what's next? Checkbox three – "Fill out the 'All About You' paper. Once you are finished, put it in the completed work basket."

I quickly fill out the "All About You" worksheet.

<u>All About You</u>

Favorite Color – *blue*

Favorite Food – *chicken alfredo*

Favorite Sport – *volleyball*

Favorite Subject – *math*

Favorite Dessert – *anything with sugar–that's pretty much all of them.*

As I place my work in the "completed work" basket, I have the biggest smile on my face. This feels so good to know what I am supposed to do. Every time I go to my checklist and mark off a task, I feel amazing!

I am finally on the last checkbox. It's the one I have been looking forward to the most! The last checkbox says – "Choose a book from the class library and have fun reading." Yippee! I finally get to select a book and read!

"Alright class, time is up," I hear Ms. Phipps say. "Please return to your seats and let's start our morning lesson."

What? Time is up! I didn't get to choose a book. Tomorrow I am going to have to focus and get my morning stuff done faster so I can read my own book.

I wonder, what will be on tomorrow's checklist? Will there even be another checklist?

Chapter 7

The BIG Idea

"Hey Riley! How was your first day of school?" my mom asks.

"Well, this morning was definitely a little bad," I replied. "I forgot to lay my clothes out and ended up quickly grabbing this outfit. Since it doesn't really match, I got a lot of weird looks and comments. Then, I didn't have time to fix my hair the way I wanted because I was spending too long trying to pick out my clothes. You already know I threw up on the baby because I was eating my food too fast. Then, I almost missed the bus. Finally, when I got to school the teacher handed me a special checklist to complete this morning. It was **really** helpful, but at first, I was so distracted by seeing my friends and checking out the classroom that I forgot to do the checklist. It was not my best morning.

"Also, did I mention I passed out because all the blood rushed to my head when I was laying on my desk looking upside down at the morning announcements? When I fell, my booty landed on my lunch and smashed it. Thankfully, my teacher was kind enough to let me have a few extra minutes to finish my checklist."

"Oh Riley Madison, I am so sorry you had a rough start to your day. Hopefully tomorrow will be better. I want to hear more about this checklist that was so helpful. What kind of checklist was it?" Mom asks.

"It was a list that had all the things we were supposed to do with our school supplies. It told us where to put our backpacks and lunchboxes, what assignment we needed to complete, and where to turn it in. Once I started reading the list and focused on all the boxes to check, my morning started going great!" I tell her.

"Mom, I just realized how much the list changed my day! I struggled all morning until I finally focused on the list. It was like a superpower! It felt like it gave my brain and body laser focus. Anytime I got distracted and wondered what I should be doing next, I just looked at my list, and then I knew exactly what to do! It was awesome!

"Mom, I have an idea forming. I think this idea is getting crazy good! Do you want to hear my idea?" I ask her.

Mom laughs and says, "Yes, Riley Madison, I can't wait to hear your crazy good idea."

"What if I make my own lists to help me stay focused?" I exclaim. "I could make a list of all the things I need to do in the morning. Then, as I complete my tasks, I could check them off and know I am getting things done and making the right choices!"

"I love that idea, Riley Madison!" my mom agrees. "Why don't you start working on your list while I get the baby up from his nap. When you finish, I can go over your list with you."

I am so excited about making my list that I start working on it immediately. I just so happened to have a marker in my hand from where Emma and I were coloring pictures on the bus on the way home.

Rather than taking the time to go find some paper, I decide to just start the list on my hand. Okay, what should be the first thing on my list? I quickly write "#1 Make my bed." I wrote pretty big, so now I use my other hand to write "#2 Put school clothes on." That hand doesn't have any more room to write, so I write on my arm "#3 Put pajamas in the dirty clothes." On the other arm, I write "#4 Brush and fix hair." The rest of my list I decide to write on my legs. By the time I am finished with all I can think of, my hands, arms, and legs are covered with my superpower list.

"Riley Madison!" my mom shrieks. "What have you done?"

"Mom, I completed my list. Isn't it great?" I say. "I think I have remembered everything."

"It sure looks like you have remembered a lot based on the writing that is all over your body," my mom sighs.

As my mom looks at the marker in my hand, she gets the weirdest look on her face.

"Riley Madison, is this the marker you used to write on your skin?" she asks.

I quickly nod my head.

"Oh no! This is a permanent marker," she gasps. "It doesn't wash off easily at all!"

"What?" I whisper. What am I going to do? I can't have my body looking like a list forever.

"How about a bubble bath?" Mom suggests. "Maybe soaking in the tub will help get the marker off your skin, but first let's write down your list on something more appropriate."

After writing down my list with Mom, I go upstairs and start my bath. I pour in the yummy strawberry-smelling bubble soap. I get in the tub and start scrubbing my skin. Wow, this marker really doesn't want to come off. After scrubbing for a while, I realize I am very tired. I decide to turn on the bathtub jets that make your bath feel like you are in a jacuzzi. I push the button and lie back in the tub to relax.

Uh oh, what is happening? The soap bubbles are getting bigger and bigger! The bubbles were only halfway up the bathtub just a minute ago, but now they are all the way to the top. Oh no, now they are running over into the bathroom floor!

"Mom! Help!" I yell.

Mom comes in and runs over to turn off the jets. We let the water out of the bathtub and get a lot of towels to wipe up all the bubbles.

After we clean the mess up, Mom looks at my skin that still clearly has purple marker all over it. She suggests that maybe a shower will help get the rest of the marker off.

I look down at the lists all over my arms and legs. Will I look like this forever?

[illegible] something [illegible] to men at the [illegible]. We're the worst [illegible] at [illegible] get [illegible] for [illegible] to make up all the [illegible].

After [illegible] When [illegible] my [illegible] help [illegible] He purple marker all over [illegible] [illegible] help get [illegible] of the [illegible].

[illegible] down at the list [illegible] arms [illegible] forever.

Chapter 8

My List –
My Superpower

Beep! **Beep! BEEP!**

It can't be morning already! I feel like I just fell asleep, and I was having the best dream! My dream was about me being a superhero! Although, I wore the craziest outfit. I was wearing a pink tutu, mismatched socks, and a t-shirt with a cape. Yikes! It was literally my first day of school outfit from yesterday.

I quickly turn off my alarm and jump out of bed. I sneak a peek at myself in the mirror to see if the list on my body has gone away.

After an overflowing bubble bath and three showers, you can still faintly see the list on my arms and legs. Mom assured me it would *eventually* go away, but it would take time and a lot more scrubbing. On the bright side, I am now super clean. I might be the cleanest I've ever been in my whole life!

Before I scrubbed though, Mom and I sat down and wrote my list on a whiteboard. It even has a dry erase marker that attaches to it. Mom said I could use the dry erase marker to actually put a checkmark as I complete the tasks on my list. She also made me promise I would not use the dry erase marker to write on my skin. Actually, I had to promise not to write on my skin ever again... with any marker.

I am determined to make this morning a better morning than yesterday. I definitely want to have more time to eat breakfast and not throw-up on my baby brother again. So, what should I do first?

I spot the list that my dad and I hung up yesterday by my door. The list has a section for my morning routine, but it also has a section for my nighttime routine. For example, the nighttime list says things like, "put homework in backpack, place tennis shoes by the door, brush teeth, and lay out clothes for school." Once I checked off all the boxes on my nighttime list last night, I went to sleep feeling good.

Right now, I need to focus on my morning list though. Let's see... #1 – Make your bed. I hurry and make my bed and put all 42 stuffed animals on top for decorations. I **LOVE** stuffed animals!

I go back and put a check by #1. The next thing on the list says "Put school clothes on". Thanks to my nighttime checklist that reminds me to lay out my school clothes, I remembered to get my clothes ready before I fell asleep last night. There's no hurrying and trying to find a great outfit for today because I laid out the perfect outfit last night. I swiftly put on my llama t-shirt and jean shorts. I even have matching socks.

I put a check by #2. I continue to follow my checklist and mark every single task off. I even have time to do a cool hairstyle. Let's see, where is my hair chalk? I quickly color the ends of my hair blue and pink. I pull it up into pigtails and am very pleased with the look.

My little brother, Lawson, comes in and asks me to make his hair blue. I color the ends of his hair blue and spike it up. When baby McGuire crawls into the bathroom, we decide to fix his hair too. We make his hair purple and spike it into a mohawk. When we show McGuire what he looks like in the mirror, he stares at himself and then starts screaming.

Dad yells, "I'm coming!"

When Dad opens the bathroom door, he freezes and stares at us. Then he picks up McGuire and starts bouncing him. It's hard to tell, but I think my dad is trying not to laugh.

"Let's head downstairs for breakfast," Dad says. "I can't wait to see what your mom says about your hairstyles."

I bounce down the stairs and check the time. Whoa! I have 20 minutes before I have to be at the bus stop. This morning is going great!

"Wow! You all have some cool hairstyles," Mom says somewhat shocked.

"Aren't they great?" I ask. "Mom, if you want your hair to have some extra color, I can fix yours too when I get home from school."

"Thanks, Riley Madison. I might let you do that," she says with a smile.

I sit down and have time to take small bites of my breakfast and listen to my dad tell silly jokes. I would tell you his jokes, but they aren't very funny. I laugh at them though because I don't want to hurt his feelings. Trust me though, his jokes are way funnier than my mom's. She can never remember the full joke and often forgets the ending, which is supposed to be the funniest part.

"Alright Riley Madison, finish your breakfast. It's almost time for the bus," my mom says.

She didn't even sound stressed when she said that. Hmm, maybe my checklist is helping her too. Or maybe, she found the checklist I made for her.

Actually, I made EVERYONE a checklist! Since my brother can't read, I drew pictures for his checklist. I even added things like, "help Riley Madison clean up her toys, play Riley Madison's favorite game with her, help make Riley Madison's bed, straighten up Riley Madison's shoes..."

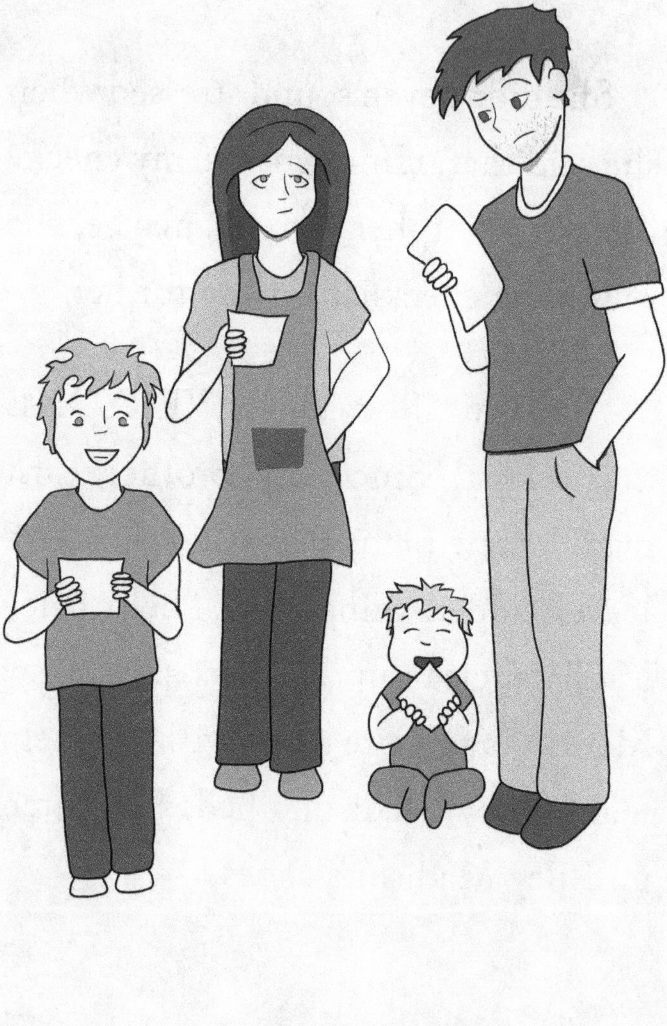

I really can't wait for Mom and Dad to complete all the tasks on their checklists. Number 9 on Dad's list is to adopt a puppy for our family. Number 7 on Mom's checklist is to take us to an amusement park.

"Okay, Riley Madison, put on your shoes and grab your backpack. Let's walk down to the bus stop," Mom says.

Since I completed my nighttime checklist yesterday, I walk with confidence over to my backpack. I know it is packed with my finished homework assignment. And since #7 on my nighttime checklist said "Put tennis shoes by backpack," I am guaranteed matching shoes today.

Mom and I don't even have to run to the bus stop. She and I get to walk like normal human beings. We even get to say hello to our neighbors and talk for a minute while we wait on the bus to get there.

As I listen to my mom talk to my neighbors, I realize she seems much more relaxed this morning. Then, I think about how I am feeling. I am more relaxed. I feel a calmness that I don't ever remember feeling on a school morning.

I think my lists really do have superpowers! I like this feeling of success and knowing I am not forgetting anything. I feel like a superhero. The lists are like my superpowers! They help me have superhero laser focus and confidence. I know that if I have the list and check it off, I won't forget anything.

I wonder if my parents will finish their lists today and have this same feeling of success? How cool would it be if I came home from school and we had a new puppy and went to an amusement park?

If that happens…these lists are even more powerful than I think!

I'll start working on some cute puppy names just in case!

Letter from
Riley Madison

Hey friends!

I wanted to let you know that my lists have helped me so much! In the story you found out that I have a list to help me remember what I need to do at night and in the morning. I also discovered that having lists in my classroom was a huge help. I even have a sticky notepad in my desk where I make lists at school. For example, if the teacher gives us 3 things to do, I write the three things on my sticky note, and then put it on my desk. Also, when my mom asks me to help with chores, I write them down on a list.

Yesterday my mom said she had four things I needed to complete before dinner. I grabbed a sticky note and wrote the four things down. Once I checked them all off, I felt such a feeling of success. I knew that when I came down for dinner and Mom asked me if I had finished everything, I could confidently say yes!

If you are like me, you have a lot on your mind, or just find that you are easily distracted. I mean, after all, we are kids. We have a lot of things to keep us busy, and it's so easy to lose our focus with things like toys, video games, television, friends… So, I hope you will try making lists too.

We can all be like superheroes and use this superpower to conquer our world of distractions. How cool is it that we get to create our superpower lists daily? So, how are you going to use your superhero power today?

Your superhero teammate,

Riley Madison

About the Author

June Akers loves working with kids. Whether it's instructing in the classroom, teaching private piano lessons, or helping her own four children navigate through life, helping kids learn and grow is a sweet spot in her life. While working with students she has come to realize that paying attention, focusing, and learning to stay on task is a real struggle for children, especially in today's overstimulating, tech-savvy world.

After 15 years of parenting a daughter with ADHD and having three very active sons, she and her daughter, Riley, have had some breakthrough discoveries. They have been life-changing in helping her very own Riley Madison learn important skills to tackle everyday life with an overstimulated brain. Can you guess who inspired this book...the one and only Riley Madison herself!

June has a Bachelor's degree in Elementary Education and a Master's degree in Instructional Leadership. June lives with her husband and four children outside of Atlanta, Georgia.

Visit her website at www.juneakers.com

About the Author

CPSIA information can be obtained
at www.ICGtesting.com
Printed in the USA
FSHW011909151220